Knick Knack Paddy Whack

Illustrated by
Christiane Engel
Sung by
SteveSongs

Barefoot Books
step inside a story

This old man,
he played one,
He played Knick Knack
on his drum.

With a Knick Knack, Paddy Whack
give a dog a bone,
This old man came rolling home.

This old man,
he played two,
He played Knick Knack
just for you.

With a Knick Knack, Paddy Whack
give a dog a bone,
This old man came rolling home.

This old man,
he played **three**,
He played Knick Knack
happily.

With a **Knick Knack**, **Paddy Whack**
give a dog a bone,
This old man came rolling home.

This old man, he played four,
He played Knick Knack on my door.

With a Knick Knack, Paddy Whack
give a dog a bone,
This old man came rolling home.

This old man,
he played five,
He played Knick Knack
as we jived.

With a Knick Knack, Paddy Whack
give a dog a bone,
This old man came rolling home.

This old man, he played six,
He played Knick Knack on the bricks.

cinema

Pizza Pirates

With a
Knick Knack,
Paddy Whack
give a dog a bone,
This old man
came rolling home.

This old man, he played seven,
He played Knick Knack by the oven.

With a Knick Knack, Paddy Whack
give a dog a bone,
This old man came rolling home.

This old man, he played eight,
He played Knick Knack as we ate.

This old man, he played nine,
He played Knick Knack all the time.

With a Knick Knack, Paddy Whack
give a dog a bone,
This old man came rolling home.

This old man, he played ten,
If you sing a bit louder,
we'll do it all again!

With a Knick Knack, Paddy Whack
give a dog a bone,
This old man came rolling home.

Instrument Families

trumpet

drums

clarinet

Musical instruments belong to different groups, or families. They are grouped together because of the kinds of sounds they make. Here are the instrument families you can see in this book:

Brass instruments have a bell-shaped opening at one end. In this book, the **trombone** and **trumpet** belong to the brass family. Other members of the brass family include the French horn and the tuba.

maracas

Woodwind instruments used to be made of wood, but now are made from metals and plastics as well. The player makes the sounds by blowing air into the instrument. In this book, the **clarinet** and the **saxophone** belong to the woodwind family. Other members of this family are the oboe, piccolo and flute.

bass

Stringed instruments are bowed, plucked or strummed to make the sounds. You can see the stringed **bass** and **guitar** in this book. Violins, violas and cellos also belong to the string family.

trombone

Percussion instruments are struck or shaken to create a sound. The family is divided into untuned (non-pitched) percussion, like the **drums** and **maracas** in this book, and tuned (pitched) percussion, such as the xylophone or timpani.

saxophone

keyboard

Keyboard instruments have bars, pipes or strings that vibrate when a player presses down on the keys. There is an **electric keyboard** in this book; pipe organs, accordions and pianos also belong to this family.

guitar

Sing Along

This old man,   he played **one**,   He played knick knack   on his drum. With a

Knick Knack, Paddy Whack   give a dog a bone,   This old man came rolling   home.

This old man, he played **two**, he played knick knack just for you . . .

This old man, he played **three**, he played knick knack happily . . .

This old man, he played **four**, he played knick knack on my door . . .

This old man, he played **five**, he played knick knack as we jived . . .

This old man, he played **six**, he played knick knack on the bricks . . .

This old man, he played **seven**, he played knick knack by the oven . . .

This old man, he played **eight**, he played knick knack as we ate . . .

This old man, he played **nine**, he played knick knack all the time . . .

This old man, he played **ten**, if you sing a bit louder, we'll do it all again!

For Sunshine Marko
— C. E.

With thanks to SteveSongs for lead vocals;
Mark Collins for musical direction, arrangements
and piano; Alex Hutchings for guitar and alto sax;
Chris Burden for trumpet; Matt Davies for trombone;
Robin Davies for principal bass; and
James Candy for drums and maracas

Barefoot Books
2067 Massachusetts Ave
Cambridge, MA 02140

Barefoot Books
294 Banbury Road
Oxford, OX2 7ED

Text copyright © 2008 by Barefoot Books

Illustrations copyright © 2008 by Christiane Engel

The moral rights of Barefoot Books and Christiane Engel
have been asserted

Musical arrangement by Mark Collins,
newSense Music Productions

Lead vocals by SteveSongs

SteveSongs appears courtesy of PBSKids

Animation by Karrot Animation, London

First published in Great Britain by Barefoot Books, Ltd
and in the United States of America by Barefoot Books, Inc in 2008

This paperback edition first published in 2011

All rights reserved

Graphic design by Louise Millar, London

Reproduction by B & P International, Hong Kong

Printed in China on 100% acid-free paper by Printplus, Ltd

This book was typeset in Garamond, Emmascript and Hombre

The illustrations were prepared in acrylics and digital collage

ISBN 978-1-84686-659-3

British Cataloguing-in-Publication Data:
a catalogue record for this book is available from the British Library

Library of Congress Cataloging-in-Publication Data is available under
LCCN 2007025046

3 5 7 9 8 6 4 2